SKYLARK CHOOSE YOUR OWN ADVENTURE® · 17

"I DON'T LIKE CHOOSE YOUR OWN ADVENTURE® BOOKS. I *LOVE* THEM!" says Jessica Gordon, age 10. And now, kids between the ages of six and nine can choose their own adventure too. Here's what kids have to say about the new Skylark Choose Your Own Adventure® books.

"These are my favorite books because you can pick whatever choice you want—and the story is all about you."
—**Katy Alson,** *age 8*

"I love finding out how my story will end."
—**Joss Williams,** *age 9*

"I like all the illustrations!"
—**Savitri Brightfield,** *age 7*

"A six-year-old friend and I have lots of fun making the decisions together."
—**Peggy Marcus** *(adult)*

Bantam Skylark Books in the Choose Your Own
  Adventure® Series
Ask your bookseller for the books you have missed

WILD HORSE COUNTRY

LYNN SONBERG

ILLUSTRATED BY SARA KURTZ

A Packard/Montgomery Book

A BANTAM SKYLARK BOOK®
TORONTO · NEW YORK · LONDON · SYDNEY

RL 2, 007–009

WILD HORSE COUNTRY
A Bantam Skylark Book / June 1984

Skylark Books is a registered trademark of
Bantam Books, Inc.

CHOOSE YOUR OWN ADVENTURE® is a registered
trademark of Bantam Books, Inc. Registered in
U.S. Patent and Trademark Office and elsewhere.

Original conception of Edward Packard

Produced by Cloverdale Press, Inc.
133 Fifth Avenue
New York, N.Y. 10003

Front cover art by Ralph Reese

ISBN 0-553-15261-0

PRINTED IN THE UNITED STATES OF AMERICA

CW   0 9 8 7 6 5 4 3 2 1

*For Casey, Anna,
and Little Joey.*

READ THIS FIRST!!!

Most books are about other people.

This book is about you—and your mare Ginger!

What happens to you depends on what you decide to do.

Do not read this book from the first page through to the last page. Instead, start on page one and read until you come to your first choice. Then turn to the page shown and see what happens.

When you come to the end of a story, go back and start again. Every choice leads to a new adventure.

Are you ready to explore wild horse country? Then turn to page one . . . and good luck!

On a crisp September morning you pull on your riding boots and begin the long walk to the barn. You can't wait to exercise your three-year-old mare Ginger.

Only two years ago Ginger was wild. During a spring storm she was separated from the band of wild horses that roams the hills and canyons around your ranch. When your father found the frightened yearling and led her to the barn, it was love at first sight. Ever since then she's been yours.

You reach the old red barn and open the door. You listen for Ginger's welcoming whinny but hear nothing. A little worried, you run to her stall. "Hey, sleepyhead, I'm here!" you call.

But the large box stall is empty, and your golden mare is gone!

Go on to page 2.

2   You run outside to the corral, but Ginger is nowhere in sight. Where could she have gone? What if she's lost or hurt—or worse?

You lean against the gate, trying to decide what to do. Two of your parents' horses trot over. It's Stormy and Flapjack, looking for treats. That's it! You can take one of them and go after Ginger.

Flapjack is a fat old quarter horse. He's steady, but he likes to take his own sweet time. Stormy is a black stallion. He's fast but kind of wild. You're a good rider, but you're not sure you can handle him outside the ring.

If you decide to ride Flapjack, turn to page 8.

If you decide to ride Stormy, turn to page 6.

4   Flapjack plods steadily along the weedy trail to Dead Man's Bog. When the ground turns soft and wet, you get off and tie the quarter horse to a tree. Then you push through a large clump of reeds.

There's Ginger, grazing at the very edge of the bog. One false step and she'll be knee-deep in mud.

Slipping the lasso over your shoulder, you run toward your golden mare. You're so anxious to reach her, you forget to look where you're going. You trip over the root of a moss-covered tree stump and fall into the bog.

Turn to page 54.

6   Stormy prances as you saddle him up. Finally you manage to quiet him, and five minutes later you're on a trail that leads to wild horse country.

You hold Stormy down to a trot for a few miles. Then suddenly he jerks his neck, nearly pulling you over his head. Before you can recover, he's galloping out of control.

Up ahead is a big stone wall. What if it's too high for Stormy to clear? He might stop short and send you crashing into the wall! Maybe it would be safer to jump off now, when you can pick a good spot to fall. But if you jump off, you'll never catch Stormy. And without a horse, how will you find Ginger?

If you hold on tight and hope that Stormy can clear the wall, turn to page 25.

If you jump off now, turn to page 13.

You saddle Flapjack, grab a lasso, and mount the gentle horse. You search around the barn for Ginger's trail, but the dirt is hard-packed, and you can't tell which hoofprints are fresh.

Suddenly you remember something. Last year when Ginger got out of the pasture, you found her munching apples in the orchard. But to get to the orchard from the barn, she'd have to pass through Dead Man's Bog.

Oh, no! What if she's trapped in the mud pits there?

If Ginger *is* stuck, you may need help rescuing her. But if you go all the way back to the house to get your parents, you'll lose precious time.

If you go for help, go on to page 10.

If you ride on to the bog, turn to page 4.

10

You're halfway to the house when you spot a strange horse trailer—with Ginger inside! You get off Flapjack, and the old lazybones heads straight for the barn. Then you go into the trailer, untie Ginger, and back her down the ramp. Suddenly a tall man with a droopy moustache appears. It's Pete, the new ranch foreman, and he's leading Samantha, your parents' prize mare.

"What's going on?" you ask.

Pete scowls. "Get that mare back inside!" he orders. "You and these here horses are going for a ride."

Your mouth drops open. Pete is stealing the horses, and now he intends to kidnap you! If you move fast, you might be able to escape. But then Pete will get away with Ginger and Samantha. If you go with Pete, you may get a chance to free the horses. But Pete may have other plans for you.

If you run for it, turn to page 14.

If you get into the trailer, turn to page 18.

Just before Stormy reaches the wall, you jump off and land safely in the thick, dry grass. The horse stops short. Then he turns and gallops back toward the barn.

As you get to your feet, a blast of wind hits you in the face, and you notice there are storm clouds gathering overhead. Suddenly the smell of burning scrub tickles your nose. You turn and see a wall of flame coming toward you. Brush fire!

You know there's a cave in the rocky hillside up ahead. If you can get there in time, you should be safe. But what if you're not fast enough? There's also a shallow stream a few yards away. If you stay in the water, maybe you'll escape the fire.

If you try to reach the cave, turn to page 20.

If you jump into the stream, turn to page 36.

You've got to escape! You slap Ginger hard on the rump. She rears up in surprise, lashing at Pete with her hooves. You take a somersault dive behind the trailer, but as you roll to your feet, you twist your ankle. The pain is so bad you can hardly stand.

"You won't get away," Pete roars, trying to grab Ginger's halter.

If only she can hold him off while you limp to the house...

Turn to page 34.

You grab the marsh grass with both fists and pull. But the grass rips in your hands, and you fall backward. Now the mud is up to your chin, and you're really scared.

"Help! Help!" you yell.

Ginger pricks up her ears and, stepping carefully, comes as close to you as she can. But her front legs sink in the muck. As she turns around to find dry ground, her tail swishes over your head. Just in time you free your arms and grab the coarse golden hairs.

Ginger shivers in surprise, but she stands still.

"Pull, Ginger, pull!" you cry.

As Ginger moves forward, pain shoots through your arms. You don't think you can hold on. Then—GLUCK!—your upper body rises out of the mud, and Ginger drags you to safety.

When you get to your feet, Ginger butts her head playfully against your chest, almost knocking you down.

"Cut it out!" you say sharply. The last thing you want is another mud bath.

Ginger backs off, surprised at your harsh tone of voice.

"Okay, girl, okay. I'll forgive you this time," you say, scratching her between the ears. "But no more wandering away from the barn! Who knows— the next time I try to save you, you might not be able to save me!"

The End

18 For almost half an hour, the trailer bumps along a dirt road. Finally Pete stops at a gate blocking a small box canyon. He unloads the horses and leads them into the canyon. Then he shoves you through the gate too. You notice that there are sheer cliffs on every side. The gate is the only way out.

Pete ties your hands behind your back. "I'll take care of you later," he hisses. Then he squats down in the dust near the gate and tilts his hat over his eyes.

Ginger and Samantha are grazing under a tree—along with six more of your parents' best horses. Pete must have been up half the night stealing them!

Pete seems to be dozing beneath his hat. This could be your last chance to escape. But your hands are tied, and you're not sure you can find the way home. To make things worse, you hear coyotes howling in the distance.

If you try to sneak past Pete, turn to page 26.

If you wait for a better chance to escape, turn to page 23.

20   You run toward the rocky hillside. The fire is so close now that you can hear it roar. You'll never reach the cave in time!

Suddenly a golden flash catches your eye. "Ginger! Ginger!" you shout to the galloping mare. Ginger swerves toward you and stops, her eyes wild with fear. You leap on her back and ride for your life.

When you're halfway home, the wind changes direction and a gentle rain begins to fall. Pretty soon you're soaking wet, but you don't care. You know the house and barns are out of danger. And Ginger and the other horses are safe!

The End

You decide you'll have a better chance of escaping if your hands aren't tied. So while Pete sleeps, you rub the rope back and forth against a sharp rock. Finally your hands are free.

Quietly you walk to Ginger's side. You're sure you can jump her over the gate. Once you clear it, you can gallop to safety. But that would mean leaving the other horses behind. If you take the jump and then circle back to open the gate, the other horses will be able to follow Ginger. But then Pete may catch you.

If you think opening the gate is too risky, turn to page 32.

If you think it's worth a try to free the other horses, turn to page 40.

23

Half scared, half excited, you lean forward in the saddle for the takeoff. Hooray! Stormy jumps smoothly over the wall.

When the stallion's feet touch the ground, you hit the saddle as hard as you can, hoping that will slow him down. Your trick works, and you draw Stormy to a halt. "Good boy," you say, patting his sweating neck.

From behind the next rise you hear a faint whinny. It's Ginger!

You could ride up to her on Stormy, but Ginger doesn't like the stallion, and she might run away. You could also approach her on foot. Ginger follows you around when you're in the pasture, but who knows how she'll behave in wild horse country. She might run away, and if you're on foot, you'll never catch her.

*If you go after Ginger on Stormy,
turn to page 28.*

*If you dismount and walk toward the mare,
turn to page 38.*

You tiptoe past Pete, squirm under the gate, and run until you can't go another step. Then you sit down to rest, struggling to remove the rope tying your hands.

OWWOOOOOO! A spooky howl sends a chill of fear up your spine. You look up and see a pack of coyotes heading straight for you.

You leap to your feet and run as fast as you can, but the coyotes force you toward the edge

of a high cliff. A few feet beyond, there is a giant fir tree. If you can reach the tree, you'll be safe.

"An easy jump," you think, leaping for the tree.

Too bad you forgot your hands were tied. For you it's

The End

You ride up the hill on Stormy. On the next rise you see a dozen wild mares. In the gully between, you see Ginger—and she's in trouble. A white stallion is nipping at her legs, trying to make her join the other mares!

Ginger neighs loudly. She tries to escape, but she is no match for the huge white horse.

Stormy neighs in return. He rears up, and his hoofs cut through the air. You realize he wants to fight for Ginger!

If you dismount and let Stormy fight, he could get hurt or even killed. But if you don't, you might lose Ginger. You think fast. What if you and Stormy circle the gully and charge the mares? If you could make them run, the white stallion might forget Ginger and go after his herd.

If you let Stormy fight, turn to page 51.

If you charge the mares, turn to page 42.

The tree stump looks pretty sturdy. You lift the lasso from your shoulder and throw. As the rope settles over the stump, you sink up to your ears in mud!

In panic you jerk the rope tight around the stump and pull as hard as you can.

Uh-oh! You must have pulled *too* hard. Helplessly you watch the rope slip off the mossy stump.

Better luck next time.

Glurp...glurp...glurp....

The End

32 You leap on Ginger's back. As she jumps the gate, Pete grabs your foot. But your boot comes off in his hands, and he sprawls backward in the dust. You can hear him cursing and sputtering as you gallop away.

After a few miles you come to a narrow ravine. A roar makes you look up. Terrified, you see a large rock roll over the edge of the cliff. Ginger rears up in panic, taking you by surprise. As you hit the ground, your ankle twists. You try to stand up, but you can't put your weight on your hurt ankle.

If you don't get out of the ravine fast, you might be buried in a rockslide. But how can you get back on Ginger when you can't stand on both feet? Desperately you look around. There's a ledge twenty feet away. Maybe you could crawl to it and take cover.

CRASH! Another rock hits the ground.

If you crawl for cover, turn to page 45.

If you try to get back on Ginger, turn to page 46.

As you reach the front door, your father and the sheriff pull up in a Jeep.

"Dad, Dad!" you shout, gasping for breath. "I twisted my ankle and Pete stole Ginger and Samantha and . . ."

"And a bunch of the other horses, too," says your dad. "Don't worry, we'll get them back."

"Pete double-crossed his partner, so his partner squealed," says the sheriff. "The state troopers are already on their way to Pete's hideout."

"I never did like his moustache," you say with a frown.

Your father smiles. "Next time I'll let *you* hire the foreman," he says. "Now let's take a look at that ankle."

The End

You dive into the stream and float on your back. When you feel the heat of the fire on your face, you pull some snake grass from the bank. Then you duck your head underwater and breathe through the hollow reeds.

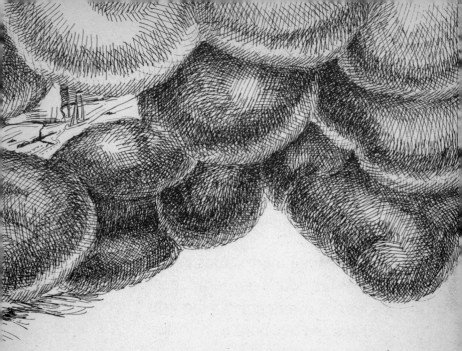

As the wind blows the fire over the stream, the water gets warm. Then hot. Then very hot.

Oh, no! You've made a terrible mistake. You don't think you can stand the heat another minute.

CRAAAACKK! The sky explodes with thunder and lightning. Rain pours down, cooling the stream. You stick your head above the water and see wisps of smoke curling up from the ground. The fire is out, but what has happened to Ginger?

Turn to page 48.

38   You tie Stormy's reins to a tree and hurry up the hill. When you reach the top, your heart almost stops.

A wild stallion is pawing the ground on a high ridge just a few hundred yards from Ginger. He rears up and neighs loudly, as if calling to her.

"Ginger! Ginger!" you shout, fighting back tears.

The golden mare stands very still. She turns to look at you, then looks back at the wild stallion. A moment later she trots to your side and stamps her hoof as if to say, "Well, what are we waiting for?"

"That's right, girl! That's right!" you say, throwing your arms around her neck. "If we don't get back to the barn pretty soon, we'll miss our morning ride."

The End

Pete wakes up as you and Ginger clear the gate. But you're determined to free the other horses, and you circle back anyway. As you lean over and knock down the gatepost, Pete grabs your arm. He's got you!

Suddenly the other horses gallop toward the open gate. Pete leaps back against the cliff, trying to get out of their way.

Too late.

"YEEEEEEOW!" he screams, holding his trampled leg.

With your parents' horses following close behind, you gallop back to the ranch. You herd the horses into the pasture. Then you and Ginger head for the house.

You're feeling pretty good. All the horses are safe. And Pete's trapped in the canyon with his injured leg. "All I have to do now is telephone the sheriff," you say, slipping off Ginger's back.

A few minutes later you return to the yard.

Oh, no. You forgot to tie up Ginger, and now she's gone again!

The End

You and Stormy circle the gully. Then you
spur him forward, shouting at the top of your
lungs. The frightened mares scatter in all direc-
tions, and the stallion canters after them, leaving Ginger far behind.

Your idea worked! You get off Stormy and snap a lead rope on Ginger's halter, standing between the two horses—just in case. Stormy tries to rub noses with Ginger. At first the mare shies away, then she changes her mind and nuzzles back.

"It's about time you two made friends," you say, patting their necks. "But did you have to scare me half to death to do it?"

The End

As you slowly crawl toward the rock ledge, you hear another rumble. Small boulders the size of beach balls are bounding down the cliff.

"Run, Ginger, run!" you shout.

Ginger rears, neighing frantically. "Not without you," she seems to say.

"Go home, Ginger. I mean it!" you scream.

The last thing you see is your golden mare galloping away.

Turn to page 52.

Standing on your good foot, you call Ginger over. Then you reach for her mane and try to pull yourself up. But you're just not strong enough. Rocks and pebbles are falling all around you now. You lean against Ginger's front leg and begin to cry.

Suddenly Ginger kneels. Of course! You taught her that trick last year. It was handy when you rode bareback and didn't have stirrups to help you mount.

Quickly you climb on her back and gallop to the end of the ravine. As you look back, half the cliff collapses in a jumble of rocks.

You reach the ranch safely and put Ginger in the barn. Now if you can only manage to hop to the house to call the sheriff . . .

Turn to page 34.

48   Dripping wet and miserable, you trudge back to the house. As you pass the barn where your father stores apples and hay, there is a loud noise. You rush inside. Hundreds of apples are rolling from the storage bin onto the floor. And there's Ginger, half-buried in fruit, munching happily away.

You don't know whether to laugh or cry. Ginger has been safe in the barn the whole time! "What am I going to do with you?" you scold. "You'll get a stomachache for sure!"

Ginger hangs her head, then drops a perfect apple at your feet. You have to laugh. "Okay, I forgive you, girl," you say to the mare. "Now let's go back to the barn, nice and slow. You've got a lot of apples to walk off."

The End

You slip off Stormy's back and he charges the white horse. For a few minutes the two stallions circle each other, snorting with rage. Then they rear up, dancing on their hind legs and lashing out with their hoofs.

Ginger comes to your side, and you watch with fear as Stormy loses ground. Then, little by little, the white stallion is forced backward. Suddenly he breaks away from Stormy and canters over to his waiting mares. As the herd moves off, he looks over his shoulder at Ginger. "Who needs you anyway?" he seems to say.

"Hooray for Stormy!" you shout as the black stallion trots up to the golden mare. Ginger whinnies loudly and tosses her head. You can't help laughing. "I'm glad you agree!" you say.

The End

52

When you wake up, you're in bed with a bandaged head and a sore ankle.

"How did you find me?" you ask your father.

"Ginger showed us the way. You hit your head pretty hard, and your ankle is strained, but the doctor says you'll be fine. We got Pete and the horses, too."

A dozen questions pop into your head. You open your mouth to speak, but your mother interrupts. "Not another word," she says. "You need to rest now."

"Aw, Ma," you protest. "It's boring to rest. I like excitement."

Your mother smiles. "I should think you've had enough excitement for a lifetime."

Your eyelids are getting heavy. "Well, maybe enough for a couple of days," you admit. Then you fall fast asleep.

The End

Yuck! The slimy mud is up to your waist, and you feel yourself sinking. You could grab a fistful of marsh grass and try to pull yourself out, but you're not sure the grass will hold you. Or you could try to lasso the tree stump. The only problem is, if you miss it the first time, you may not get another chance.

If you grab the marsh grass, turn to page 16.

If you try to lasso the stump, turn to page 31.

ABOUT THE AUTHOR

Lynn Sonberg, a graduate of the University of Chicago, has worked as an acquiring editor of adult and juvenile books at several New York publishing houses. Today she divides her time between Sag Harbor, Long Island, where she writes, and New York City, where she operates a book packaging and editorial service.

ABOUT THE ILLUSTRATOR

Sara Kurtz was born in Canada and studied fine arts at the University of Windsor, in Ontario. Now living in New York City, she produces filmstrips for children as well as illustrating children's books.

Now you can have your favorite Choose Your Own Adventure® Series in a variety of sizes. Along with the popular pocket size, Bantam has introduced the Choose Your Own Adventure® series in a Skylark edition and also in Hardcover.

Now not only do you get to decide on how you want your adventures to end, you also get to decide on what size you'd like to collect them in.

SKYLARK EDITIONS

☐	15238	The Circus #1 E. Packard	$1.95
☐	15207	The Haunted House #2 R. A. Montgomery	$1.95
☐	15208	Sunken Treasure #3 E. Packard	$1.95
☐	15233	Your Very Own Robot #4 R. A. Montgomery	$1.95
☐	15308	Gorga, The Space Monster #5 E. Packard	$1.95
☐	15309	The Green Slime #6 S. Saunders	$1.95
☐	15195	Help! You're Shrinking #5 E. Packard	$1.95
☐	15201	Indian Trail #8 R. A. Montgomery	$1.95
☐	15191	The Genie In the Bottle #10 J. Razzi	$1.95
☐	15222	The Big Foot Mystery #11 L. Sonberg	$1.95
☐	15223	The Creature From Millers Pond #12 S. Saunders	$1.95
☐	15226	Jungle Safari #13 E. Packard	$1.95
☐	15227	The Search For Champ #14 S. Gilligan	$1.95

HARDCOVER EDITIONS

☐	05018	Sunken Treasure E. Packard	$6.95
☐	05019	Your Very Own Robot R. A. Montgomery	$6.95
☐	05031	Gorga, The Space Monster #5 E. Packard	$7.95
☐	05032	Green Slime #6 S. Saunders	$7.95

Prices and availability subject to change without notice.

Buy them at your local bookstore or use this handy coupon for ordering:

Bantam Books, Inc., Dept. AVSK, 414 East Golf Road,
Des Plaines, Ill. 60016

Please send me the books I have checked above. I am enclosing
$_____ (please add $1.25 to cover postage and handling). Send
check or money order—no cash or C.O.D.'s please.

Mr/Ms _____

Address _____

City/State _____ Zip _____

AVSK—6/84

Please allow four to six weeks for delivery. This offer expires 12/84.